The Rainbow Feelings of Cancer

A Book for Children Who Have a Loved One with Cancer

CARRIE MARTIN AND CHIA MARTIN

ILLUSTRATIONS BY CARRIE MARTIN

HOHM PRESS • PRESCOTT, ARIZONA

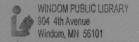

Self-portrait with purple hair, age 6

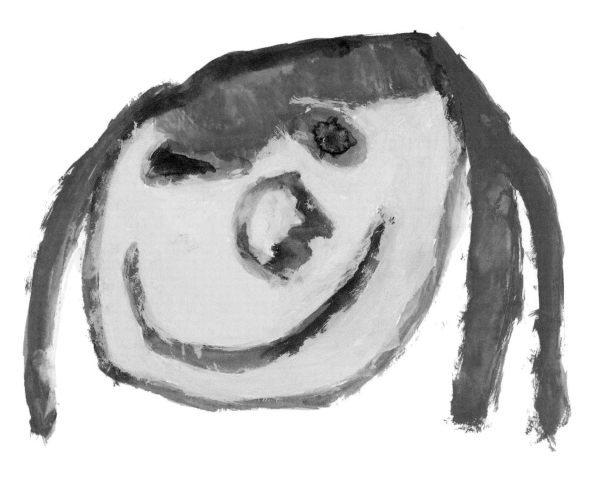

Library of Congress Cataloging-in-Publication Data

Martin, Carrie, 1990-
   The rainbow feelings of cancer / by Carrie and Chia Martin.
      p. cm
   Includes bibliographical references.
   Summary: A ten-year-old girl tells of the many feelings she has regarding her mother's cancer.
   ISBN 1-890772-16-X (hardcover)
   1. Cancer--Juvenile literature. [1. Cancer. 2. Diseases. 3. Emotions.] I. Martin, Chia. II. Title.

RC264.M374 00
362.'96994'009--dc21

HOHM PRESS
P.O. Box 2501
Prescott, AZ 86302
1-800-381-2700
www.hohmpress.com

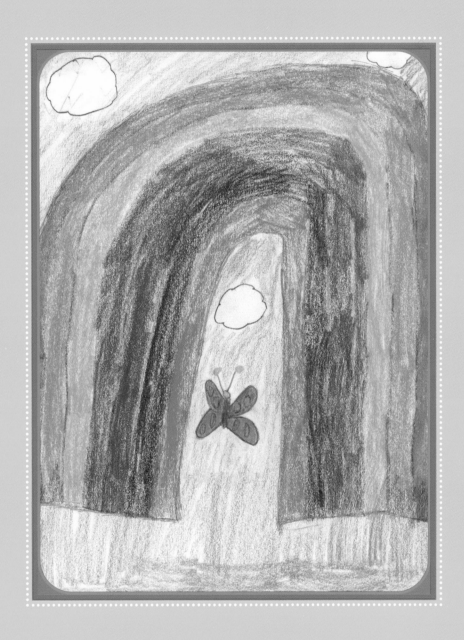

**To all parents and children
who have stood beneath this rainbow.**

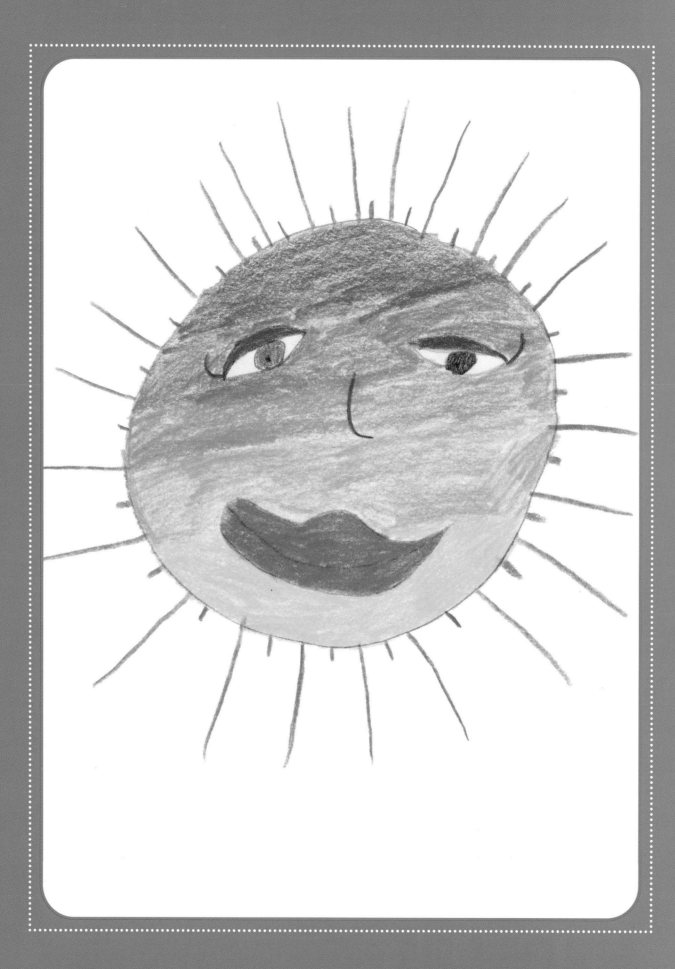

Carrie's Note

Hi. My name is Carrie.
I am ten years old.
This book is about me and my feelings.
When I was seven, my mom got cancer.
She still has cancer, but is doing lots of things to try and
    make it go away.
Kids whose parents have cancer have lots of feelings.
Some of the feelings I had before my mom got cancer.
Some of the feelings I hadn't really noticed before.
Some feelings like sad and mad got stronger.

These are some of the feelings I have had.
Maybe yours are the same; maybe different.
Maybe reading about mine can help you with yours.
Drawing my feelings has been a big help to me and my mom.
One thing I know for sure—cancer brings out lots of feelings.

Chia's Note

Creating this book was one of the best things Carrie and I
    ever did together.
It unfolded because we both needed it.
I hope it can serve as an inspiration for you, whether or
    not your lives have been touched by cancer.

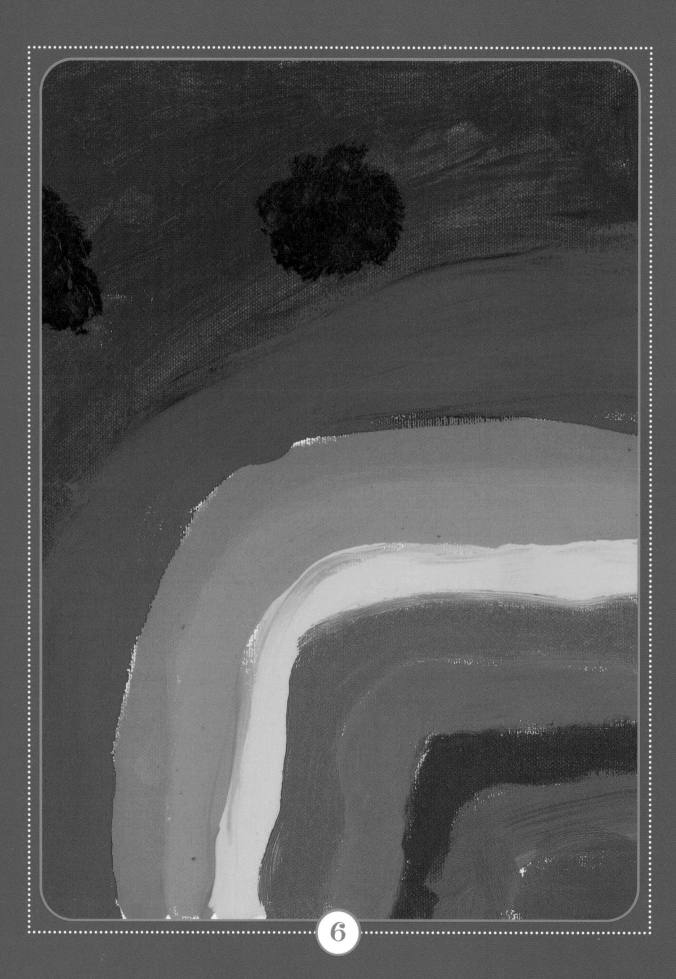

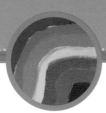

First, I want to say one thing about rainbows.

Have you ever noticed that a rainbow sky is usually blue and clear on one side and black and stormy on the other?

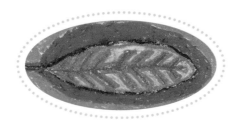

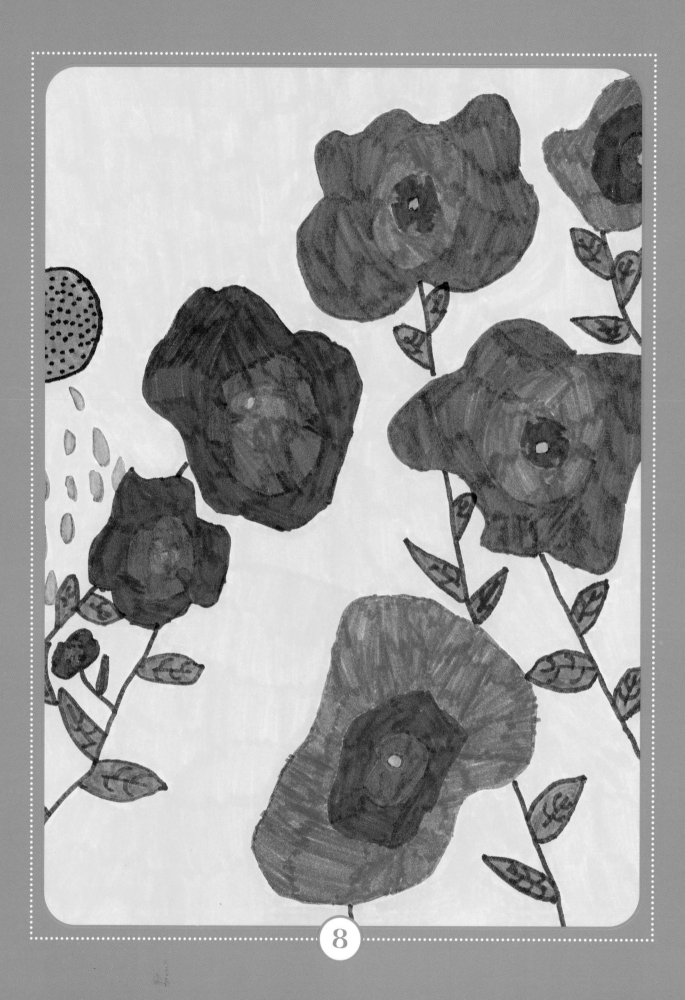

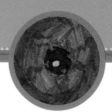

When my mom first got cancer, I had never heard of cancer before. I thought there might be something I could do to make it go away.

I felt

helpless.

Now that I'm older I know I can't make the cancer go away, but I can do things to help my mom like water the pansies.

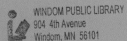

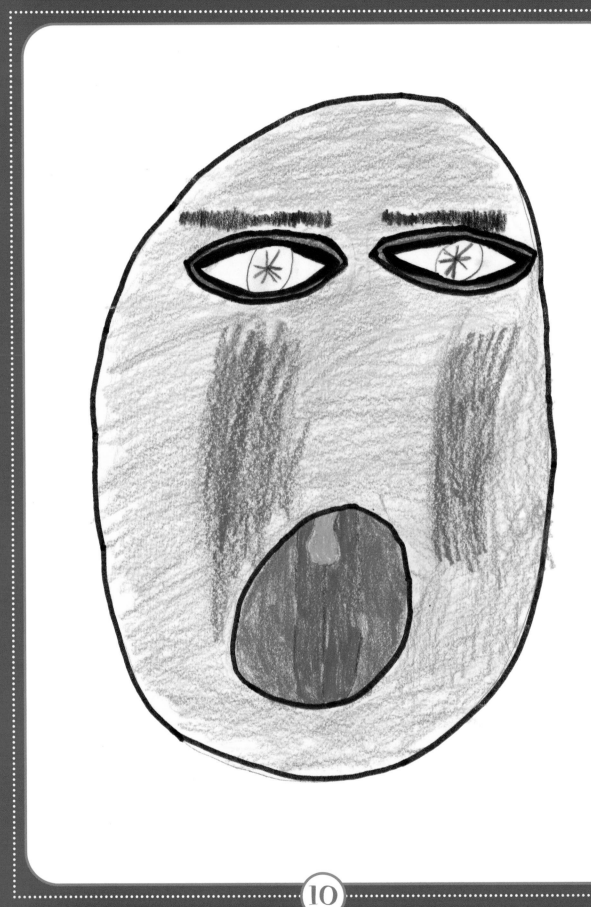

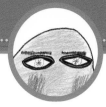

This is my

angry

picture.

Some days I am very mad about cancer.

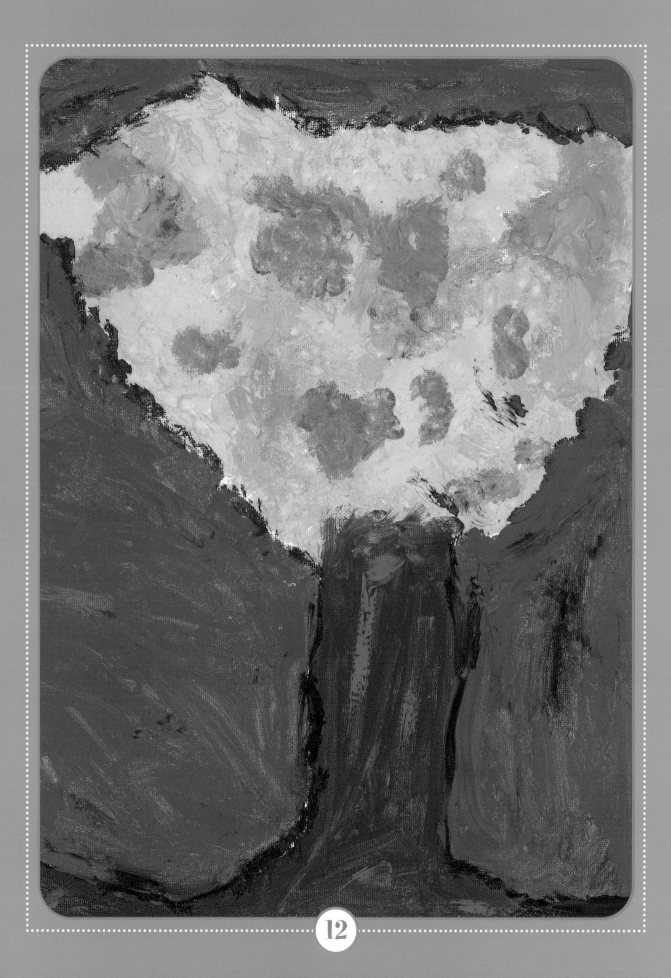

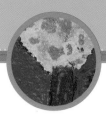

This is my best tree painting ever.

One thing my mom tells me is that
I'm my own person.

She reminds me that my life is very full and
that her cancer is just one part of it.

That helps me feel

strong and sturdy

like this tree.

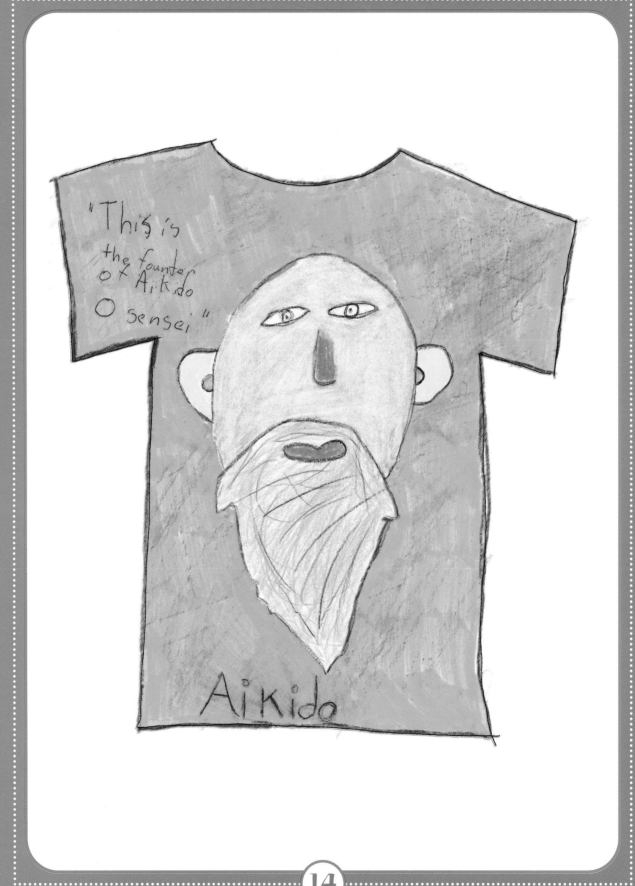

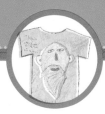

I think the hardest thing for me
is all the things my mom can't do
that she used to do, like take me
to Aikido and go to the movies.

The Doctor

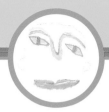

My mom goes to lots of doctors.

One part of me likes them because
I want them to help my mom get better.

Another part feels like they get
to see my mom more than me.

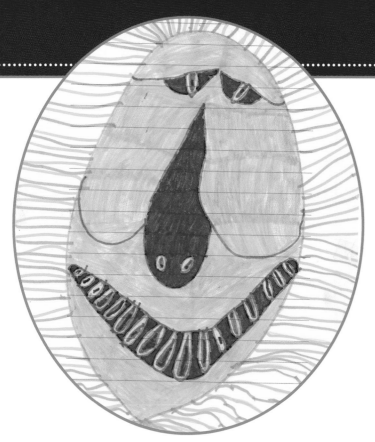

Shonook the Goblin

These are my two pictures about

s c a r e d.

As you can see one looks fierce
and one looks friendly.

One night my mom had to go the emergency
room. That was very scary. It felt like
Shonook was creeping around. I was
very glad when mom came home even
though I still get scared sometimes.

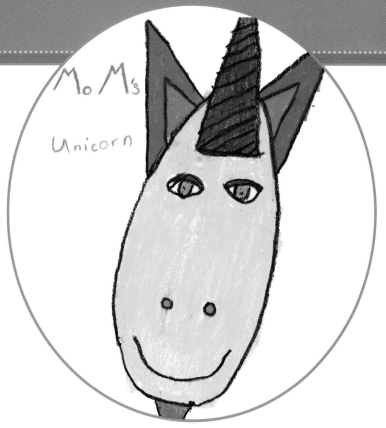

Sharmane the Unicorn

When mom snuggles me at night
she tells me stories of Sharmane.

They help me feel less scared and also

safe.

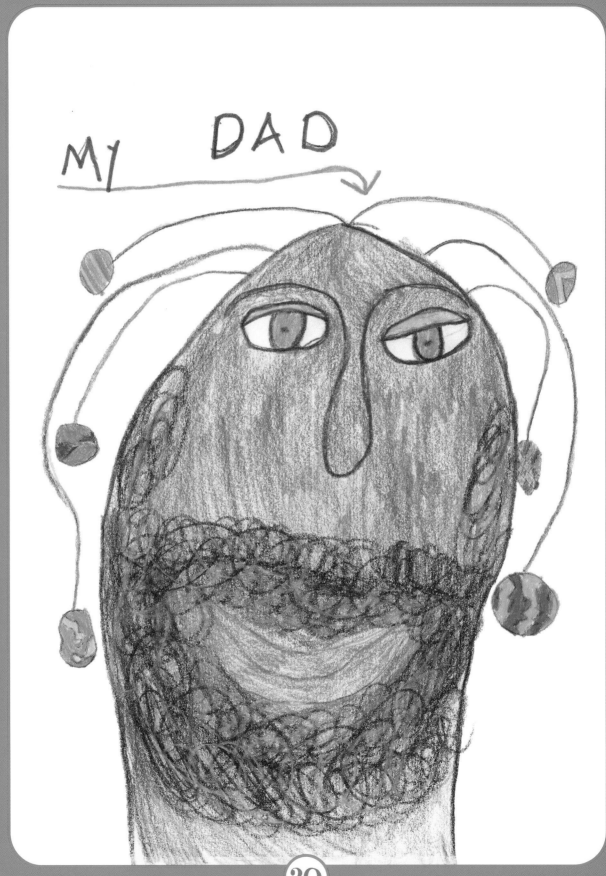

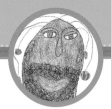

It's nice to have someone you can talk to.

It's also nice to have someone
who doesn't expect you to talk.

My dad is this person for me.

He knows how to listen.
He's someone I am

comfortable

with.

That's a very important thing.

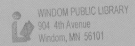

MY
MoM's
FEET

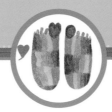

These are my mom's feet.
She loves to have her feet rubbed.

I always pour out gobs of massage
oil and that makes us laugh.

Mom reads to me while I rub her feet.

Mom says that

laughing

helps her immune system.

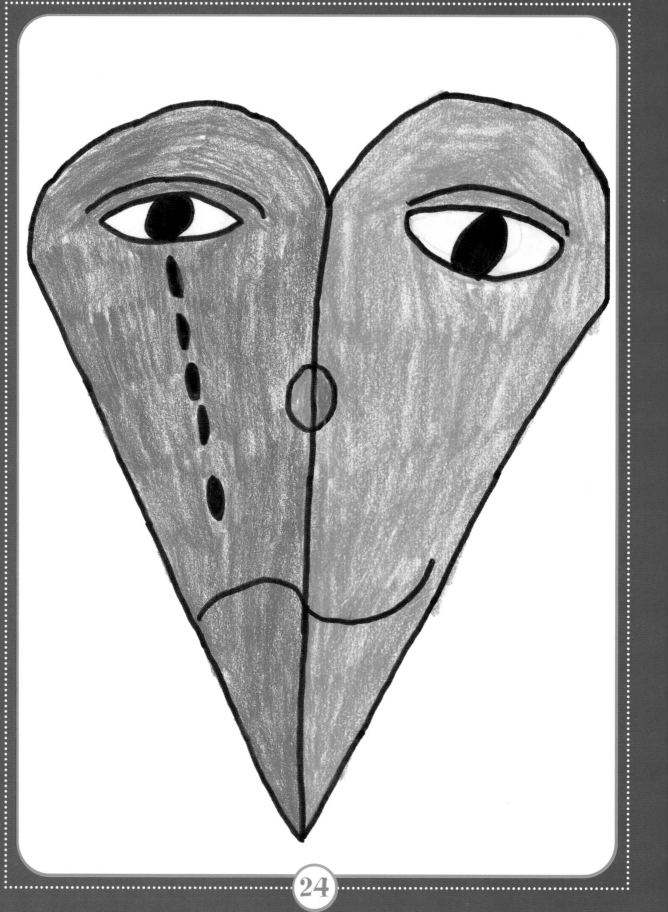

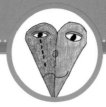

HAPPY

and

sad

at the same time.

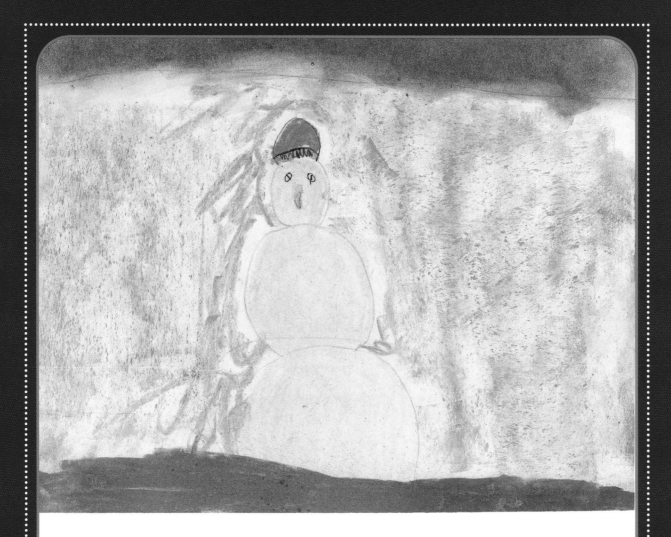

This is my melting snowman.
My mom says he looks

I don't feel lonely because I have a
loving family, but I bet some kids feel
lonely when someone they love has cancer.

He's melting. That's good for the flower bulbs
and spring grass. Some good things come out
of cancer too. Those are harder to explain.

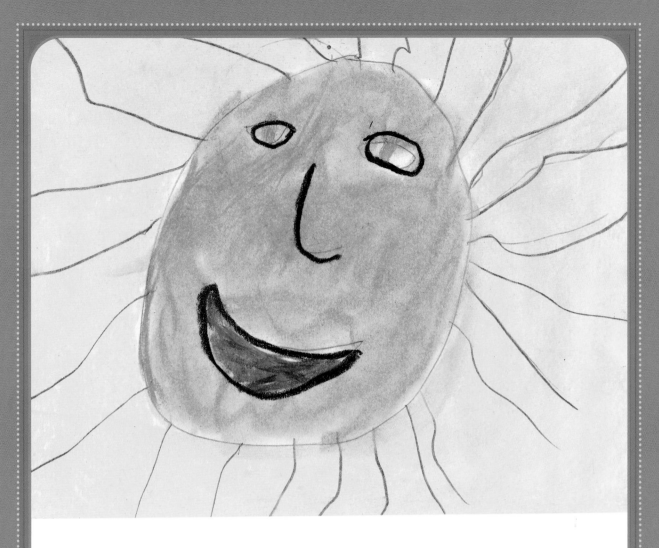

I call this

Sunny Day

because:

Mom felt good enough to
take me to my violin lesson.

The doctor said mom is doing better.

My sister did a very silly dance for me.

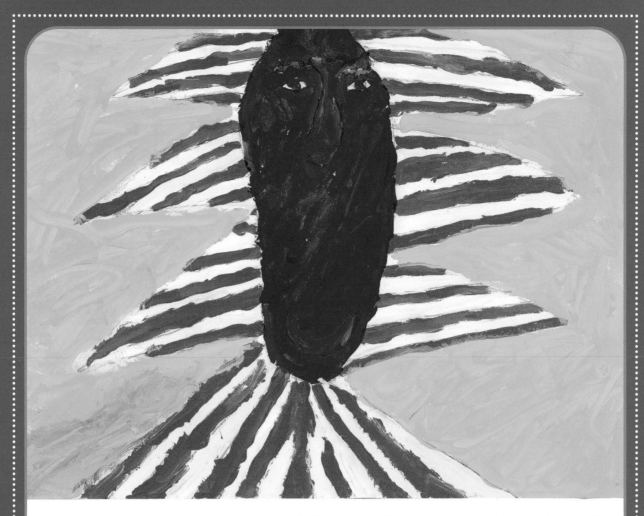

Self-portrait with red and white striped hair, age 10

I have a few more things to say about cancer.

I told my mom that maybe I used too many bright and happy colors. I don't want some other kids whose moms or dads or friends have cancer to think it is la-de-da.

Because cancer is no fun. But these are my favorite colors and also, even with my mom's cancer, I am

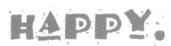

HAPPY.

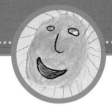

FOLLOW YOUR HEART

If you look closely at my picture which I drew
one year ago you can see I have lots to love.

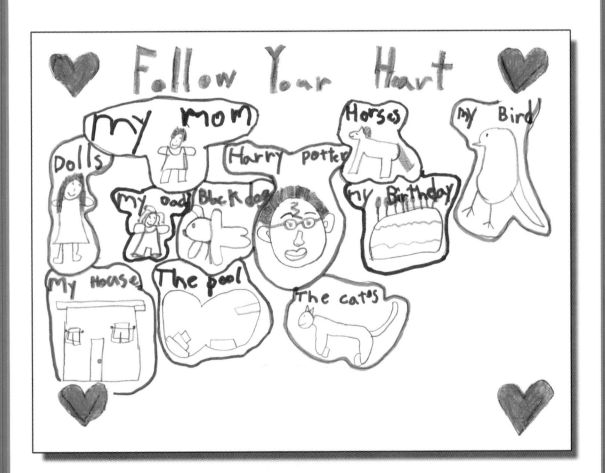

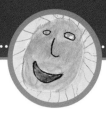

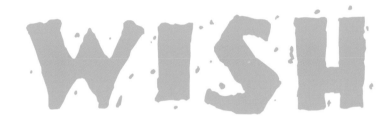

My mom and I wished on the same star.
Mom wished my wish to come true.

I wished the same wish I wish on every
candle, every fountain, and every star.

I bet you can guess why my wish is.

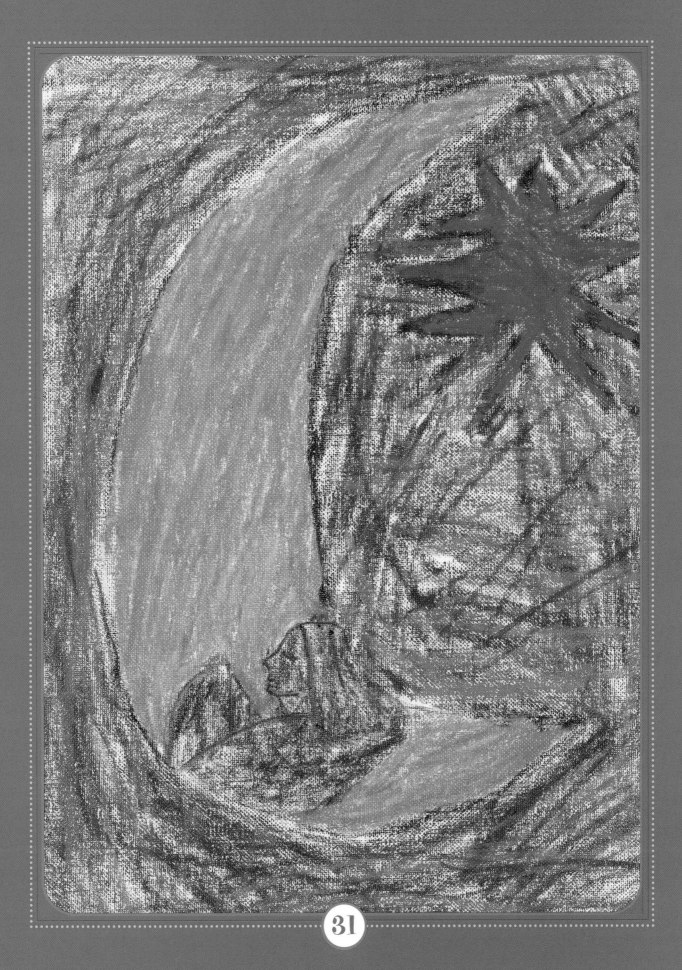

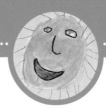

Here are some books we found helpful.

For Children
Sammy's Mom Has Cancer
by Sherry Kohlenberg
Gareth Stevens Publishing, 1994

Becky and the Worry Cup
by Wendy S. Harpham, M.D.
harper Collins Publishers, new York, 1997

Paper Chain
by Claire Blake, et al.
health Press, 1998

For Adults
When A Parent Has Cancer:
A Guide to Caring for Your Children
by Wendy S. Harpham, M.D.
Harper Collins Publishers, New York, 1997

Writing Your Way Through Cancer
by Chia Martin
Hohm Press, 1999